T0147093

# Where
## *Columbines*
# GROW

KATHERINE SPARACINO

WESTBOW
PRESS®
A DIVISION OF THOMAS NELSON
& ZONDERVAN

This is a work of fiction, except actual places are used in a fictional setting. Some of the characters, names, incidents, organization and dialogue in this novel are either the products of the author's imagination or are used fictitiously The dates are correct.

WestBow Press books may be ordered through booksellers or by contacting:

WestBow Press
A Division of Thomas Nelson & Zondervan
1663 Liberty Drive
Bloomington, IN 47403
www.westbowpress.com
844-714-3454

Cover artwork by Rosemary Rank

ISBN: 978-1-6642-4678-2 (sc)
ISBN: 978-1-6642-4679-9 (hc)
ISBN: 978-1-6642-4677-5 (e)

Library of Congress Control Number: 2021920576

Print information available on the last page.

WestBow Press rev. date: 11/02/2021

Dedicated to my husband who has
supported me in all my endeavors.

# CONTENTS

## Chapter 1

## FALLING ROCK

ROM the high mountains, cascading streams forming crystal waterfalls forced cold, clear water to rush along the narrow, rocky bed through the lush hidden valley. The brilliant sun shone in a vibrant blue sky, yet the air felt cool as summer drifted into autumn. Beavers brought aspen branches to the nearby wetlands to build their winter lodges. Greedy hummingbirds and bees attacked flowers for food before they fled from the long winter cold. Songbirds filled the sky as they searched for bugs and seeds along the river's edge. Eagles soared in great circles above the steep cliffs. Falling Rock heard their piercing cries as he washed his hands in the creek and stood up to stretch. His statuesque form cast a long shadow over the water. A chipmunk chased a black-tailed squirrel over his feet.

As he surveyed the majestic snow-covered peaks, he couldn't help but thank the Great Spirit for this bountiful place. In the distance, low, heavy dark clouds began to smother the mountaintops. As he lifted a string of trout out of a pool, he noticed sparkling yellow flakes in the black sand and wondered, *How long will it be until the white man comes and desecrates this precious, sacred valley?* They were already nearby, scouring the streams and turning the earth inside out, and he knew his way of life was about to change. Word spread at annual festivals his tribe enjoyed with the Utes. Great powwows held in the valley would cease. Yet, despite knowing the future, he would be powerless to stop it.

He mounted his horse and slipped away into the trees. The Arapaho Indian would hunt in the forests above the river until deep snows, or man, kept him out of the valley.

# Chapter 2

## WATER

"WATER!" Rebecca MacKenzie called out to her two older brothers working in the cornfield. The small young woman carried the wooden buckets with ease; her loose auburn locks swirled in the breeze, and her green eyes blazed.

"Boy, that will sure taste good now." Frederick, hot and weary, took the dipper and poured water over his blond head.

"You missed your mouth." Matthew laughed, shaking his brown hair. "Thanks, Li'l' Sis." He took a big drink. "How's Ma today?"

Rebecca set the buckets down and stretched her shoulders. "She's up. Pa has her bundled in her quilt and put her in the rocker on the porch."

"I still think it would be best to take her out west for the prairie cure." Frederick wiped off his face and neck.

"You only say that because you don't like farming." Matthew propped his hands on his hips.

"Well, you don't like it either. Plus, it seems a waste to have all our corn crop go into the making of bourbon whiskey."

"You know, we do live in Bourbon County, Kentucky. And since the panic in 1857, that's the best price we can get. Besides, you know Pa won't give up the farm unless Ma wants to."

Rebecca mimicked her ma. "All my babies were born here," she said, clutching her hands to her heart.

"Anyway, it would be for good for her, and for all of us, to get a fresh start." Frederick picked up the hoe.

"Maybe Daniel will change their minds when he gets back from medical school." Matthew angled his tool.

"I'd like to go out west." Rebecca sighed. "I'd love to do nothing else but raise horses."

"Good luck with that!" Matthew swung the handle over her head.

"Hey!" Rebecca grabbed the bucket and threw the rest of the water onto him. "I'm sure not going to marry a farmer!" Stomping off, she could hear Frederick laughing.

Approaching the porch, she heard Ma coughing and saw Pa sitting nearby with a cup of tea; his ashen face was filled with worry. The doctor's tonic wasn't working. Rebecca whispered a prayer: "Father God, please help us find a way to care for Ma. And if it be your will, open up the door for us to go out west."

At noon, the boys came in for dinner. The oldest brother, Joe, and his wife, May, came over with four-year-old Andrew, who busied himself on the porch, showing Grandma his bug collection.

"I have a telegram here from Daniel." Joe waved the paper. "He'll be coming home tomorrow on the afternoon train."

"Oh, that's wonderful!" Rebecca was delighted. "That should make Ma feel better, having him home again."

"I also brought the newspaper dated January 5, 1859." Joe handed it to Frederick.

"This is just what I've been waiting to hear!" Frederick grinned and read the headline to his siblings: "Gold Discovered in Colorado Territory."

"Maybe that's the ticket to get Pa to change his mind about going west," Matthew speculated. "We're older now, and it might help Ma too. Besides, this farm hasn't made any money since the panic."

"And then there's talk of the war," May, who had been a schoolteacher, offered. "I sure wouldn't like to see any of you go off to fight for slavery. We don't even have slaves."

"Anyway, it's up to Pa," Matthew said, resigned.

"What is?" Joel MacKenzie asked, coming into the kitchen and guiding his wife, Ruth, to her chair at the table while Andrew jumped onto May's lap.

"Gold's been discovered in Colorado Territory," Frederick announced.

"And Daniel's coming home tomorrow," Rebecca added.

"I see," Pa murmured, and he lowered his head for prayer. Ruth began coughing again.

# Chapter 3

## DECISION

"KIDS!" Joel MacKenzie shouted over the cacophony. "We've got to get some matters settled."

May grabbed Andrew, who was running around the table, and tried to quiet him on her lap while she sat next to her husband, Joe.

Frederick and Matthew stopped teasing their sister, Rebecca, who sat next to her mother, Ruth.

Daniel stood by his father with a stack of papers in front of him. When everyone became still, Joel sat on the other side of Ruth.

"I've done extensive research," Daniel said. "And if we can sell the farm and leave by June, we can make it to Colorado by fall."

Frederick jumped up. "So we *have* decided to go out west?"

"What we've decided," Joel stated firmly, "is going to be what's best for your mother." Ruth coughed quietly as she shivered in a quilt.

"In medical school," Daniel continued, "I studied a lot about the prairie cure for consumption, and I think it would be the best thing for Mother. This humid climate keeps her congested, and she needs to get somewhere drier at a higher altitude. And since you boys"—he looked directly at Matthew and Frederick—"seem to have the gold fever, I think we should try going out west. We will sell the farm, purchase covered wagons, and completely move ourselves and our belongings."

"What about our horses?" Rebecca's concern quieted the room again.

"We'll take what we need to make the trip, but the thoroughbreds will stay here until we can make provisions for them. We'll send for them later. They can come by train to Denver City."

"We're going west!" Frederick punched Matthew on the shoulder, and Matthew returned his gesture.

"Boys!" Joel commanded. Looking at his eldest son, he said, "Joe, we haven't heard from you yet."

Joe stood up, hanging on to the squirming Andrew. "May and I have talked it over, and we think we can start a store anywhere we go. We already have enough staples and foodstuffs in reserve to begin with. We would just need to build a place with a storefront on the ground floor and our housing above."

"Ruth?" Joel tenderly took her hand. "Do you think you can make such a long trip?"

She nodded. "I'm not any good here," she said, inciting another round of coughing.

Rebecca sprang up. "I'll make you some tea, Mother."

# Chapter 4

## THE JOURNAL

REBECCA hummed as she brushed her horse, Butterfly, and spoke gently to her. "You're such a beautiful horse, my lovely dearest. I can trust you to take me anywhere. And you know what? We are going to go out west after all!" She heard footsteps behind her and turned around. "Daniel!"

"Hey, Li'l' Sis. How's Butterfly? Ready for a long journey?"

"Oh yes! I think she'll do just fine."

Daniel held out a small brown paper package. "I got this for you before I came home from school."

She grabbed the package out of his hands, and ripping off the paper. "Oh, Daniel! It's so beautiful!" Her countenance glowed. The small book was covered in red velvet, with her name embossed in gold letters: *Rebecca Ruth MacKenzie*. The pages were embellished with gold. She gingerly fingered the lettering and smooth velvet. Inside the cover was an inscription: "*To my dear Li'l' Sis. From Daniel, with all my love, for your birthday, 1859.*" Flipping through the pages, she said, "But there's nothing in it."

"It's a journal, silly." He playfully thumped the back of her head with his hand, jerking her forward. "You're supposed to fill it up. Write about our trip out west or whatever you want."

"Thank you ever so much." She embraced him. When they separated, she wiped tears from her eyes. "It's the most beautiful thing I've ever received."

"You're welcome." He kissed her forehead and, smiling, walked away.

# Chapter 5

## THE CROSSING

REBECCA climbed down from the wagon, stretched, and took a deep breath. *Oh, the air is so nice here.*

She had never imagined how difficult the trip would be and what hardships they would face: the lack of privacy, the search for water in a desert, and a confrontation with Indians. Papa had been a good negotiator and had been able to trade goods in order to keep the stock and guarantee their safety. *Well, I suppose it could have been even worse than that.*

Caring for her mother made the trip more demanding. But Ruth was the reason they had come out west. Despite the jostling of the wagon and the extreme weather, she did seem to be doing better. Even Daniel confirmed she was coughing less, which indicated improvement.

Rebecca unhitched the horses and cared for them while the boys set up camp. Papa brought Mama's rocker out and settled her next to the fire. Andrew helped his father, Joe, collect firewood and buffalo chips, and May cooked dinner over the open fire. Tomorrow night, they would be in Denver City to spend the winter. Her brothers would scout up into the mountains to find a suitable place to live and look for the alleged gold.

Once everyone was settled, the moonless night became quiet and dark. As Rebecca snuggled into her blankets, the sky grew brilliant with tiny lights. She saw the starry cloud of the Milky Way stretched out across the horizon. A blazing shooting star dashed out of sight. "Dear Lord, lead us in thy will," she prayed, and then she went to sleep.

# Chapter 6

## THE JOURNEY

REBECCA kept a record of the trip in her journal:

On April 3, 1859, we sold our hundred-year-old Kentucky farm to embark on the twelve-hundred-mile journey to the Colorado Territory. The new owners will allow us to board our horses for the time being.

We purchased and loaded four wagons for the trip, along with spare wheels, provisions, tools, and supplies. Mama and Papa ride in the back of Daniel's wagon, which carries the medical equipment and a hospital bed. Joseph, Matthew, and Frederick drive the other wagons, each carrying extra food and water barrels. Of course, I can also drive a wagon, but I mostly wrangle the stock and ride my horse, Butterfly. Our foreman, Jonathan, has come along too.

We had to cross the Ohio River on a raft, one wagon at a time, to get to the rendezvous in St. Louis. Then we joined a wagon train that got us to Independence, Missouri. However, they turned north to follow the Oregon Trail. We could've gone southwest on the Santa Fe Trail, which would have taken us to Pikes Peak and the gold rush. Faced with the hot, flat prairies of Kansas Territory and the threat of Indians, we decided to join three other families at Portsmouth and follow the path of the planned Kansas Pacific Railway line along the Smoky Hill River. This took us directly to Denver City, where we arrived in September.

Denver City is not much more than a black dot in a barren brown dust bowl. Gold was discovered last year at the confluence of Cherry Creek and the South Platte River, where a rudimentary settlement has been established. We rented a building where we can wait out the winter. Daniel, Matthew, and Frederick went up into the mountains, following Clear Creek.

# Chapter 7

## ASPEN TREES

ASPEN leaves in blazing gold declared September's arrival as the three brothers began their arduous trek up Clear Creek Canyon. Pack mules resisted and had to be coaxed along the difficult trail.

Daniel spoke first. "Just think." His voice was wistful. "Someday there may be a train up this way or at least a road."

"I guess if there's enough gold, it could be feasible," Matthew added. "I sure hope this is worth the effort."

For now, animal tracks and litter from mountain men marked the way. It took them a week to travel the twenty-five miles from the newly established town of Golden to the settlement at Idaho Springs. Leading the animals through icy waters, they had to make frequent stops to avoid hypothermia. Other areas were wide enough for them to walk along the edge. In the distance, they saw a prospector panning for gold in the muddy water; they stopped, out of sight, watching and waiting. The narrow riverbed was lined with men on both sides. "I guess we're too late," Frederick said with a moan.

Matthew turned around and began tugging at his mule. "Let's try the other channel."

That way was even harder, creeping along the tops of the rugged, steep canyon walls they couldn't climb. Shaded rock grottos were filled with crystalized stalactites in frozen waterfalls. In some places, the river water was so deep they had to swim beside the mules, holding on to the packs. They made slow progress, and all the while, the weather got colder. There was no evidence anyone else had gone that way.

They woke up one morning with their oilcloth tent covered in snow, and the bank of the river was freezing up. "I sure wish I knew where we were going," Frederick said, shaking the snow off the tent.

"All I know is we've got to keep moving," Daniel said, packing the gear. "We can't risk frostbite."

"Always the doctor." Matthew chuckled.

By noon, the canyon widened out into a valley. Fresh snow glistened on top of the peaks; hoarfrost in a field had melted to reveal wet knee-high grass. The river they'd followed was fed from a shimmering lake at the foot of a cliff they had to go around. The valley widened as they proceeded, moving through underbrush.

On the northwest side, a large, beautiful creek pushed its way downstream with a clear and rapid current; surging waterfalls descended from high peaks to join it. Beaver dams dotted the water line, and animal trails skirted the marshy banks. A rich green valley perfect for grazing lay along the eastern edge of the creek, possessing fertile soil. Its dense foliage and wildflowers nodded in the breeze as the frost melted. The land was well watered and clothed with luxuriant herbage.

"Boy!" Matthew exclaimed. "Rebecca should see this! It would be great for a horse pasture. It's too bad we had to leave the family behind in Denver City."

"We had to find the land first," Frederick reminded him. "And it looks like we found it!"

The steep slopes surrounding the valley were thick with pine and aspen trees. Looking southwest, the men could see to the pass where the water originated. "That's mighty high up there," Matthew muttered.

"A virgin land seemingly untouched by human hand; such loveliness—where angels might recline," Daniel mused, and his two brothers stared in amazement. "What? I read that in a book somewhere."

Another stream came rushing from the southeast and merged with the river in the meadow. Sand, pebbles, and small rocks graced the bottom, glittering in the sunlight. "Let's stop here," Frederick said, and he began unloading the mules.

"Any Indian signs?" Daniel reminded them of the danger.

Falling Rock stood among the trees, watching. *Looks like the time has come.* He reported back to his tribe that the white men had plenty of supplies with them. Many braves wanted to kill them, but Falling Rock's wisdom prevailed. "That will only bring us trouble." They decided to wait and observe the activity until the snow came.

The brothers worked the confluence, panning the black soil and seeing tiny gold flakes swishing in the water. They tried for two days, disturbing the wildlife, going up and down the waterways, looking for the source. On the morning of the third day, a cry of "Gold!" echoed through the surrounding mountains. Frederick and Daniel ran to Matthew's side, where they saw small gold nuggets scattered in the spring-fed eastern runnel.

They climbed up the high piney ridge, following it to the point of origin. There they found just what they were looking for: an outcropping of blossom rock. They began to dig around it. They double-teamed on a hand drill to make holes large enough for blasting. Making progress of only a couple of feet per day, they made a cave large enough to walk into.

Daniel left to go report back to the folks in Denver City before there was so much snow that he wouldn't be able to get out of the canyon.

It was late October and was colder outside than inside the cave. Matthew and Frederick continued working the veins in the rock walls, knowing they were now snowed in until spring. They had to cut timber to shore up the sides of the mine as they dug deeper into the mountain. "Wow," Frederick murmured, "I thought farming was hard."

# Chapter 8

## CUNNING

MATTHEW and Frederick came to the mouth of the cave they had been drilling and found the valley blanketed in snow. "Boy, that sure is pretty," Matthew said with a whistle.

"Yes, but it's also very cold out there!" They dumped their buckets of rocks and debris and went back inside. "It's warmer in here."

Frederick picked up a hand drill and placed the tip against a crack near the small vein, and Matthew struck the end with a mallet. A quick turn by Frederick and Matthew struck again. They continued until they'd made a hole large enough for a charge of black powder. After adding a fuse and lighting it, they stepped out of the cave until the smoke cleared.

"I wonder why we haven't seen any Indians," Frederick said.

"Count your blessings! They've probably been around all along. They're very cunning, you know."

Taking their lantern, they ventured back into the cave and found a large deposit running all through the rock.

"Woo-hoo!" They both celebrated.

"Didn't I tell you?" Matthew said. "This beats farming any day."

"It sure does, but it's still really hard work. I've got blisters from the drill."

"I'll take it for a while," Matthew offered, handing Frederick the mallet.

"I wonder if Daniel made it back to Denver City and when the family will get here."

They labored through the winter, working in the mine and cutting timber for shoring and housing. They took turns going hunting.

One day they noticed Falling Rock's footprints in the snow. Matthew said, "Someone knows we're here."

"Yes, but he hasn't shown himself." Frederick looked around in all directions. "We're being watched but not attacked."

# Chapter 9

## THE MEETING

*S*PRING thaw arrived, and water began to flow, when Frederick decided to follow the stream above the mine. He packed his panning tools on his back so he could carry his gun and a walking stick. The trek was rocky and wearisome. Every time he got tired, he would stop and pan. He found a few flakes but knew there was more gold up ahead. The land leveled off, and coming into an open meadow, he discovered Indian teepees. He stood frozen at the edge of the field.

Falling Rock advanced toward him with armed and angry warriors following him. He raised his right hand, both to greet Frederick and to stop his braves from attacking. He noticed the backpack and asked, "Gold?"

Frederick was thankful he had learned some of the Arapaho language before leaving Denver City. Even though he was startled and shaking, he didn't raise his gun. "Uh, yes," he stammered.

"Come." Falling Rock directed all the men to sit around a fire. Frederick had seen natives before but not this many. It appeared Falling Rock was their leader, and would obey his commands.

"Our ancestors came to these mountains to live in peace with our Ute brothers." Falling Rock spoke in his native tongue. "This hidden valley you've discovered was our sacred meeting place. Now we hear rumbles where the white man destroys the land, searching for yellow rocks."

"They call that place Central City," Frederick interjected. "Many more white men will continue to come seeking their fortunes."

Falling Rock nodded in understanding, saddened. "They are insensitive to the wonders of nature around them and do not perceive the forests and life that surround them as blessings from the Great Spirit."

"Most white men," Frederick added, "say the Indian wastes the land by not using the full potential of all its resources."

"We are guardians and stewards of the land," Falling Rock continued, "using only what little we need. The whites ravage everything in their path and leave only destruction. The land cries."

Frederick felt remorse at the thought that his own family would do the same. In defense, he offered, "It is true we came here to look for gold. But we also found a place to live; to grow; and to raise horses, crops, and children. We hope that the way we develop the land will not destroy it but change it for the better."

Falling Rock was silent, contemplating the words. He'd never met a white man face-to-face until now. He'd only seen what they had done. Yet he hoped Frederick was someone he could trust, and perhaps Frederick could be a contact between his people and the settlers.

The sun slipped behind the western mountain, and Frederick decided to leave. He would take Falling Rock's message back to his people. "Stay here for now," he encouraged the tribe. "Let's see what will happen." He shared a peace pipe before departing.

# *Chapter 10*

## DENVER CITY

REBECCA sat in front of the fireplace, trying to get warm. In spite of the drier climate and powdery snow of Denver City, it was a long, cold winter without three of her brothers. She often wondered how they fared up in the mountains. Had they found any gold and land to settle? Could they make a living raising horses? Sighing, she opened her journal and thumbed through the pages.

> Day 57. I climbed off the wagon and stretched, noticing the different fragrances of flowers not found back home and the odors of the sweaty men and horses. Even the red mud of the river near where we camped had a stench. This trip has been much more difficult than I anticipated. We've experienced extreme heat and drought this past week, along with severe, stinging sandstorms. That was the worst! Sand in my hair and clothes. It even sifted into the water barrel. And poor Butterfly! Her beautiful blonde coat and white mane caked with sand. It was even more dreadful than the choking dust or crippling mud, the

aftermath of bizarre purple lightning and torrential rains. Jonathan helped get the wagons free of the muck by laying branches in front of the horses to walk on while the men pushed, and May and I pulled. Mother seemed better today, watching from a safe distance.

A sudden knock on the door startled her, and she dropped the journal. "Who is it?"

"Daniel, and it's cold out here!"

She loosened the latch, and he scrambled by, tossing in bags and slamming the door as quickly as possible.

"Oh, Daniel!" She embraced him. "We've been wondering what happened!"

"Let me warm up first." He took Rebecca's chair by the fire, and she noticed she was no longer cold.

Hearing the commotion, other family members came into the room. Ma was first, with a squeal of delight and a smothering embrace.

Joel slapped him on the back. "Good to see you, Son," he said.

"Danny!" little Andrew shrieked as he jumped into his uncle's arms. He was the only one to get away with calling him Danny.

Joseph and May stood back with arms locked and watched as the scene unfolded. May was expecting a second child.

Rebecca handed Daniel a cup of hot coffee. "Well? What's happened?" she prodded.

"Never much for patience." Daniel nodded and winked at his older brother. "Well"—he drew the word from a deep breath while Rebecca fidgeted—"we did find some land." Rebecca gasped. "And some gold."

Everyone erupted in excitement. There were dozens of questions at once: "How much? Where? How far is it? Can we all live there?"

Daniel held up a hand to silence the tumult. He gave Andrew a big hug and set him down, got up, and gathered his bags to spread them out on the table.

The first bag contained samples of gold ore sparkling in pieces of quartz, gold flakes in dark sand, and small gold nuggets. "This is a sample of what Matthew and Frederick have discovered so far. I've been to the assayer; this is worth almost two hundred dollars. I filed two legal mining claims for them at the courthouse."

"Wow," the others murmured in unison.

"The land lies in a wide, flat valley surrounded by mountains covered in trees. Clear Creek runs through the middle of it, with other streams feeding it from high snowfields. There's enough for each of us to file a homestead claim, which we'll need to do tomorrow. Since Li'l Sis is not yet twenty-one, I thought maybe Pa and Ma could file for her. I'll put one in my name and another in yours." He nodded at Joseph.

"So how much land is that?" Joseph asked.

"One hundred sixty acres each for the three claims, along with the eighteen-dollar filing fee. So fifty-four dollars for four hundred eighty acres, almost two square miles. Just about the size of our farm back home. We'll need to live on it for five years, build residences, and grow crops to prove up on the claims."

"I'm sure we can do that," Pa said.

"I wanna raise horses!" Rebecca whined.

"You can do both." Joseph spoke up. "May and I will have our hands full with a store and the children."

"I figure," Daniel continued, "the boys have two mining claims. We get the homestead claims, and then we all work together. There's fish in Clear Creek and wildlife for meat until we can get our cattle herd started."

"That sounds wonderful," Ma spoke dreamily.

"It's so beautiful, Mother." Daniel took her hands. "Plenty of flowers and birds. And the scenery is magnificent, like nothing I've ever seen before. It will be a lot of hard work at first, but it sure will be worth it. We have to live on the land for five years, making improvements, and then it's ours."

"Tell me, Son." Papa was serious. "Did you see any Indians?"

At the end of April, the MacKenzie family joined a group of wagons to go into the canyon. They would build a road as they traveled.

Rebecca looked toward the snow-covered mountains to the west and wondered what lay ahead just beyond the sunset.

# Chapter 11

## ARRIVAL

REBECCA led the team of horses out of the canyon and stopped the wagon in the open meadow beside a silver lake. "Oh my!" She couldn't believe her eyes at the wonder and beauty of it all. Turning in all directions, she inhaled the fragrances and listened to the sounds of wildlife. Patting her horse, she said, "Butterfly, we're home."

Daniel rode up beside her. "This is it," he said, waving an arm around the area. "This land by the lake is yours for the horses. I recorded your homestead in Pa's name since you're under twenty-one. You'll have to grow hay and some kind of food, but we can fence the rest of the property so the horses have room to run. You'll live here with Pa and Ma as partners in one homestead."

"Oh, it's too good to be true." She leaped with excitement. "Where's the mine?"

"Up there." He pointed southeast. "Can you see the cave? In fact, here come Matthew and Frederick now."

"We heard you coming!" Matthew said. There was a joyous family reunion with many hugs and tears and even laughter. Matthew and Frederick were delighted in the improvement in their mother's health.

"Well done, boys," Pa said. "This location is perfect for all of us."

The wagons were moved into place to designate the three homestead claims. Since Frederick and Matthew held the mining claims, they would live together. Joseph and May would occupy a homestead on the other side of the lake, where the land was drier and more level, setting up a store with housing above it. Daniel's doctor's office would be close by, with sleeping quarters in the back. Everyone would work together for the five years necessary to prove up on the claims.

Matthew and Frederick had begun building a large cabin to house everyone during bad weather until construction on the other buildings could be completed. They built a corral for the horses, a barn, a smokehouse, and a bunkhouse for the hired help. They had seen bears, moose, and mountain lions near the mine, and they hunted deer and elk in the thickets and trees.

They cut lumber from the edges of the forest rather than taking it out of the middle, which left more pastureland available, and replanted along the way. Dead trees were used for firewood.

The work was hard but rewarding. They knew they could have a bountiful life here, with a bright future on rich, fertile land. The other folks who had traveled with them picked out spots where they would settle.

As the family sat around the campfire one evening, Rebecca asked, "Have you seen any Indians?"

"Only one around here," Frederick answered. "He's an Arapaho named Falling Rock. I've met his tribe, who live up higher in the mountains. We've been learning his language and teaching him English."

"Any signs of hostility from him?" Pa was wary.

"I don't think so. He said the braves wanted to kill us, but he stopped them and said it would only cause trouble."

"Still, I think we should be prepared for trouble anyway. Let's keep the rifles always loaded and close by. We shouldn't have to wear our hand guns but they should be kept loaded too."

By the end of autumn, the big house was completed, and everyone moved in. Ma was feeling much better, and her cough was nearly gone. She worked in the cabin with May, cooking, washing, and caring for the children. Andrew gathered firewood and enjoyed the freedom of running around outside and playing in a gentle channel of Clear Creek with his dog, Mutt, who had been found on the trail. He stayed out of the main current, with Mutt watching for snakes. He couldn't wait for it to snow.

One day Papa and Rebecca were digging trenches near the lake to bring water to the house, when they unearthed a hot mineral spring, which formed a large pool. It was exciting, as it meant no more hauling water from the creek or heating it over a fire.

Daniel worked out of his wagon, where he kept his medical supplies, while erecting his office and looking after a settler soon to deliver a baby.

That was when Falling Rock came.

Rebecca was impressed with his imposing appearance; his long, braided ebony hair; and his rugged features. He nodded as he met each family member, but he stared at Rebecca, the last one introduced. His black eyes bore deep into her soul. Flushed with embarrassment, she returned his gaze, and a sweet calmness washed over her.

"And this is our baby sister, Rebecca," Matthew said.

Falling Rock nodded as Papa cleared his throat.

"You stay winter?" the Indian asked. "Very cold. Snow deep. You know," he said, looking at Matthew and Frederick.

"Yes," Matthew said.

"But we can work inside the mine all winter, where it's not as cold," Frederick added.

Falling Rock nodded, turning slowly, and looked at every member of the family. He knew other white people were settling in the area, with more coming. He didn't know how long he would be able to keep his tribe away or when the white men might try to drive them out. For now, they just kept moving higher into the mountains. "May Great Spirit bless you." He passed a hand over the family, raised it in salutation, and was gone.

"I think that went well," Daniel declared.

That winter, Daniel and Joseph helped their brothers in the mine. The work went faster, but hand-drilling became tedious. They came up with several nuggets but nothing big or substantial, as they'd hoped.

Papa and the women stayed in the cabin on stormy days with Andrew and his baby sister, Sarah, who had been born on the trip up from Denver City. They made plans to start planting in the spring, as well as making clothes, drying local berries, and smoking meat. May and Joseph designed the store. As they worked throughout the winter, Rebecca could still feel the penetrating eyes of Falling Rock. She decided to write a letter to her friends left behind in Kentucky.

The winter was mild, and a trail carved out through the canyon brought other people into the area.

# Chapter 12

## THE LETTER

TO my dear friend Elizabeth,

How I miss you so!

We finally arrived at the homesteads in June, placing our wagons in designated areas according to the map Daniel filed with the territory agency. I live by a lake with Mama and Papa and have plenty of land for my horses.

Several waterfalls flow down the pine-covered mountains, forming the lake and feeding into the river. There's also a hot mineral spring nearby, so we don't have to heat water for baths! We also built a greenhouse for vegetables.

There are many varieties of wildflowers and birds, none like we had back in Kentucky. And hummingbirds! I've never seen so many different kinds all in one place. I'm hoping to get a book for my birthday so I can begin to identify them.

This birthday will be my official coming-of-age party. I'll be twenty-one and recognized as an adult. Mama and May are planning it, but I wish you, Priscilla, and Deborah could be here. I don't have any friends yet, so it will be family and the ranch hands who work for Papa, including Jonathan.

I'm not sure how I feel about Jonathan. He's nice enough to me and assists me with the horses and all, yet I can't help but sense it's all a show. It's as if he has some ulterior motive. I guess I'll have to wait and see if his true colors come out.

Oh, and I met a local resident. Remember how I told you that while crossing the prairie, we traded with Indians so they wouldn't attack us? Well, this Indian is an Arapaho and calls himself Falling Rock. He's the leader of a small band who live in the mountains just above this valley. He has the most gorgeous ebony-colored hair, black eyes, and bronze skin. When he looks at me, I feel like he's searching into my soul for something. It's not in a threatening way. More like curiosity. Yet he has really penetrated into my heart, and I can't stop thinking about him! It seems so silly to me that we could ever have anything together. He lives with his tribe, and I live here. And I've heard of trouble from white girls living among Indians. He rides an Appaloosa horse every time he comes to visit and looks like he can handle horses well. I doubt he'd ever consider living with us. But I still wonder anyway.

May had another baby! A girl they named Sarah. Andrew was disappointed it wasn't a boy, but I'm sure that over the course of time, there will be many boys.

This area has become a town, Maysville, named after my sister-in-law, and Papa became the first mayor, although it won't be official until Daniel and Joseph register it in Denver City. That's when they'll go for supplies and mail this. There's a mining town between here and Denver City called Golden, so they may not have to travel so far for the mail.

You are in my thoughts and prayers. I love you very much.

*Rebecca Ruth MacKenzie, 1861*

*S*he wrote copies of the letter, with variations, to send to her friends Priscilla and Deborah and could hardly wait for them to be posted.

Times were exciting for Rebecca, who was anticipating her party, probably the last one she would have. Birthday parties would be for the children from now on.

When the big day came, everyone dressed in their fanciest clothes. Even the cowboys polished their boots and cleaned their hats. Jonathan Adams, Abe Wheeler, and Stan Ferguson stayed in the background while Rebecca opened her gifts.

"I got just the book I wanted!" she squealed, holding up the *Encyclopedia of Rocky Mountain Wildlife*. She also received a copy of Lt. John C. Fremont's result of his expedition along the Oregon Trail, published in 1843, which had become a common travel guide for most pioneers.

She got a red silk dress made by her mama, which had a white lace collar and cuffs and mother-of-pearl buttons running down the front and around the sleeves. "Oh, Mama!" She embraced the dress and Ruth. A dark blue dress came from May. Her brothers gave her simple things: a piece of gold ore from the mine, a tablet of writing paper, and an artist's book for drawing, along with a supply of wax-based colored sticks.

Jonathan cleared his throat and stepped forward with a gift. "I made this myself," he said, handing it to Rebecca. It was in a small canvas bag, not wrapped like her other gifts.

She gently took out a leather-riding crop with a braided handle. "That's nice," she stammered, knowing she would never use a crop on Butterfly. "Thank you," she said without making eye contact.

There was a knock on the door, and in stepped Falling Rock. Jonathan retreated to the back of the room with his friends, watching Rebecca's expressions carefully.

"Falling Rock, I'm so glad to see you." She didn't embrace him, as she wanted to.

"You birthday. We no do, but …" He handed her an animal skin.

Her hands trembled as she withdrew a leather thong with feathers and small blue stones woven in. "Oh, Falling Rock, thank you!" Tears glimmered in her eyes, while Jonathan's eyes narrowed sharply.

As Falling Rock rode back to his tribe, he couldn't stop thinking about Rebecca, envisioning her amber hair and vivid green eyes. She blocked out all reasoning. He hadn't seen those colors in a woman. *I can't have a white girl in camp, and I certainly can't go live with one.*

He didn't have experience with these kinds of emotions. The feelings overwhelmed him. Usually, if the Indians had a fancy for someone, they made a trade with the woman's father. Yet he had never taken a wife. He urged his horse to go faster, hoping the thoughts would flee. Then he had an idea, which would take careful planning.

# Chapter 13

## SPRING

*S*PRING arrived with a flurry of building activity, farming, and birthing. Butterfly had a colt. Rebecca named him Waterfall.

Matthew and Frederick went to the Denver City stockyard to arrange for wranglers to drive the horses and cattle up Clear Creek Canyon. They also went to the county recording office to list Maysville as a town in Clear Creek County. They got ledgers so folks could start recording mining claims and logbooks for town management entries. They also bought a current 1861 newspaper, which contained an article about mining for silver and news of the civil war breaking out in the east.

The town was growing fast. Settlers had come, following the stock. Houses and buildings were going up all over. The forest was rapidly receding.

Supplies were plentiful now, so Joseph quickly finished the store building, where his family could live upstairs. Daniel was making house calls, delivering babies, seeing patients in his office, and going directly to the sites of injuries.

Everyone helped with the homesteads. Barns and corrals were built, and the ground was tilled for hay and potatoes. Vegetables were growing in the greenhouse. Townsfolk boarded their horses on MacKenzie property. Everything seemed to be progressing as expected.

Then, one day, two men with pack mules disappeared while following the southern creek Frederick had traversed when he first met the Indians. The mules came back to the town without their packs. Frederick led a search party, but there was no trace of the men. Their disappearance remained a mystery and was recorded in the log.

A town meeting was held. Some of the settlers blamed the Indians for the two missing men and readied for a fight. Mayor MacKenzie warned everyone of impending danger and told them not to wander off alone. "I think we'd better stay out of the higher mountains for now," he said. Daniel kept records of births and deaths and of the missing.

A woman, Virginia Brown, came to town to start a school but was swept away in the high current of Clear Creek while washing her clothes.

A mine explosion trapped four. Rescue parties were able to reach them, although two were dead.

Rebecca, Papa, and her brothers finished the outbuildings before the first snowfall. Crops of hay and potatoes were harvested. Everyone waited to see if Falling Rock would come again. He did not.

Rebecca wondered why she felt sad at his absence. She could still see his eyes, but the feeling she'd had was drifting away with the falling snow.

# Chapter 14

## HARD WINTER

T HE snow continued to fall. Rebecca didn't mind going out and caring for the horses, feeding them and mucking out the stalls. At first, she didn't mind the cold. They had winter in Kentucky, but never like this. She and papa tried to keep up on shoveling paths from the house to the barn, tying a guide rope at each end. The ranch hands stayed busy feeding the cows and keeping ice off their noses, while maintaining a steady supply of chopped wood for all. Horses kept warm in their stalls.

The temperature continued to fall.

Frederick and Matthew worked in the mine. Joseph and Daniel constructed a sleigh to get around town which Butterfly enjoyed pulling.

Daniel reported it was 40 degrees below zero. Mrs. Johnson, who had been walking home from the store got lost in a blizzard and was found frozen to death, 30 feet from her front door. People were encouraged to stay indoors, or inside their mines where it was warmer, at least 50 degrees above zero.

By December Rebecca knew the road up Clear Creek canyon to

Maysville was closed. There were breaks in the storms where the sun's brilliant reflection nearly blinded folks but the temperature would only rise to zero. Small groups of men would set out to hunt meat, but game became scarce. Food was in short supply. The town was beginning to show signs of despair and people worried.

In January, the snow depth was over six feet in places that had not been cleared. Falling Rock came to town. He stopped at Joseph's store and was directed to the MacKenzie cabin.

Rebecca opened the door and stared into those dark black eyes. She quickly shut the door as Falling Rock came inside, shaking off the snow. She didn't break her gaze.

Falling Rock turned to Joel MacKenzie. "Snow deep, very cold. You good?"

"Yes, we're fine here. How are your people?"

"No game. Must go farther to hunt. You come?"

"I'm sure my sons would like to go."

"Would you like some coffee?" Ruth asked, offering the chair by the fire. He nodded and sat down.

Joel held out his pipe and they smoked in silence while Falling Rock drank the coffee. He smiled at Ruth in appreciation.

"Next break in snow we go." He looked at Rebecca. "You have plenty food?"

Startled, she blinked like she had just now seen him. "We're doing well." The glow from the fire highlighted his features. She spoke in short, quick breaths. "We found a –" not sure if she should tell him, "hot mineral spring – and made a – a greenhouse. We have food growing there now, and we have cattle for meat."

He nodded. "Yes. Sacred Water. My people use in ceremonies."

Rebecca flushed embarrassment. "Oh, we didn't mean to take that away fr…"

He waved his arm to stop her. "Use water, it good."

Joel stood up when Falling Rock did. "I see horses," he said. "You have good place. Do well. Take care of land." He looked directly at Rebecca. "Watch over L'il Sis." He'd heard her brother speak that phrase before. Rebecca felt faint.

"Would you stay for dinner?" Ruth urged.

"No, return to my people. I get brothers for hunt."

"That will be fine." Joel extended his hand in friendship. Falling Rock returned the gesture, then glanced at Rebecca again, his black eyes deepened, penetrating her soul. He raised his hand, nodded slightly and left.

Rebecca sat down and exhaled. Her father looked at her. "He seems to be a fine man, different from the Indian stories we heard back east."

"I think we are the first white people he's ever known," Ruth said.

"Probably so."

In town, news of Falling Rock's appearance spread like wildfire and settlers became anxious and apprehensive. Some of them realized they had taken the land from the Indians and worried they would start a war.

Mayor MacKenzie reassured them at the next town meeting that the natives were peaceful, only trying to survive the winter like everyone else. Some thought a militia should be formed. "Let's wait until spring," the mayor suggested, "but I don't think we'll need one." He closed the meeting.

The winter hunt was successful. Joseph and May were able to provide meat for the town until spring. They also sold some produce from the greenhouse.

A few townspeople were aware that it was Falling Rock who had helped in the hunt, and started to feel more at ease about the Indians. Others were extremely cautious, even to the point of hating them. They felt *entitled* to the land as part of their *Manifest Destiny.*

A fierce, shrieking wind roared through the valley uprooting trees and demolishing structures. A stable was blown over killing one horse. A new house under construction disappeared entirely. The wind lasted for two days and nights gusting up to gale force. Snow drifted into mountainous piles. Activity in town came to a standstill.

All of the MacKenzie family stayed together in the big house. Matthew and Frederick didn't work in the mine. Joseph closed the store. Daniel went on calls, when folks could get to him. The ranch hands did the outdoor work, performed in short intervals, and stayed in the bunkhouse most of the time. Card playing became quite popular, and Rebecca had a few games to share. Papa taught Andrew some rope tricks and how to tie knots. May remained close to the fireplace, as she wasn't feeling well. Everyone longed for spring.

# Chapter 15

## ANDREW

NINE-year-old Andrew MacKenzie had many adventures with Mutt, exploring wetlands and wooded areas, searching for animals, and chasing rabbits. Sometimes Aunt Rebecca would go exploring with him, riding her horse, Butterfly. Mutt would warn Butterfly of a snake or a hole she might step into.

Andrew liked springtime best, when everything started to bloom, and babies were born. He loved watching the beavers and ducks teach their young how to swim in a quiet pool off the main current of Clear Creek. His mother was due to have another baby also.

Andrew was a good big brother to three-year-old Sarah, but he was glad to get away from the crybaby girl. She mostly stayed in indoors, doing girl things, such as playing house. Andrew wanted a brother, a friend to play with. He didn't know that his mother's pregnancy was having complications.

Mutt was chasing a rabbit, when he ran into a cactus and filled his face with needles. Andrew carried him home and arrived just as his uncle Daniel closed the door to his parents' bedroom. Andrew didn't see his father, but he heard his mother crying. He laid Mutt carefully on the floor.

"What is it?" Andrew asked.

"Your mother did have a boy," Daniel replied.

Andrew drew an excited breath.

"But I couldn't get him to start breathing." Daniel paused. "He's dead."

Andrew's face turned pale, but he really didn't understand. He'd seen dead animals before but had not experienced a death this close to him.

Daniel sighed and hugged him. Andrew didn't cry.

Mutt whined, and Daniel said, "Guess we'd better take care of Mutt here."

They went outside.

The shock didn't come to Andrew until the funeral. He was disturbed by seeing his parents cry, and that upset him into tears.

There were now five in the small cemetery of Maysville: the teacher Virginia Brown, who had drowned in Clear Creek; Mrs. Johnson, who had frozen to death; the two miners and Baby Boy MacKenzie.

# *Chapter 16*

## JONATHAN

*J*ONATHAN Adams, tall and slender, a sun-darkened cowboy with sandy-colored hair, had been a faithful employee of Joel MacKenzie for several years. He'd worked cattle on their Kentucky farm and assisted with the horses. Joel had promoted him to ranch foreman before they left for Colorado with two other hands, Abe Wheeler and Stan Ferguson. He executed his duties faithfully and to the letter.

Making the arduous trek with the family, he had pitched in when wagons were stuck in the mud, fixed broken wheels, crossed rivers, hunted stray stock, and searched out hidden water holes.

Jonathan's generous smile was reserved only for Rebecca. He had used extra precaution in taking care of her along the treacherous journey, maybe because she was the youngest or a girl or because he loved her. For whatever reason, he worked untiringly on constructing the buildings in Maysville where the MacKenzie family would live and work as he continued to care for the livestock.

He met Rebecca one morning while she was coming into the corral. "Good morning, Rebecca."

"Hello." She saddled Butterfly and hung the leather crop on the saddle horn.

Jonathan removed his hat to wipe his brow and retied the kerchief around his neck. He stood for a moment, surveying both the beautiful countryside the MacKenzies had chosen for their ranch and their beautiful daughter. He offered her a dipper of water out of the bucket.

"Thank you. How are the colts?" She petted the nearest one.

"Fine. Stan, Abe, and I are going to the stockyards to pick up the new horses. They should be in Denver City from Kentucky by now."

"Oh, that will be great! We're doing pretty well, aren't we?"

"Yes," he said. *But not good enough!*

As he watched her ride away, he wondered what Falling Rock had to do with her attitude. She had become cool and indifferent toward him since they'd arrived and started the town.

Jonathan didn't like Indians, especially after their encounter with them on the prairie. He was suspicious and cynical. He resented the relationship developing between Falling Rock and the family, especially Rebecca. It might jeopardize his plan of marrying her and inheriting the homestead. Somehow, he would think of a way to stop him.

# *Chapter 17*

## FREEDOM

IN May, Jonathan traveled Clear Creek Canyon with Abe and Stan to bring up more horses. They also brought news that the Civil War was raging in the east.

Rebecca and her papa watched as the stock were put in a corral. The MacKenzies now had two dozen horses, and three of the mares were in foal.

"It takes such a long time to build up a horse ranch," Rebecca complained to her father one day.

"We're doing quite well, considering there was nothing at all on this land when we arrived three years ago."

"Now that Jonathan is back," she continued, "I feel so confused. On the trail, when we were all coming out here, I thought I liked him. He is very nice. But I like Falling Rock too."

"You've got to realize that he's of a different race and culture and is the leader of his people. I don't think they would ever accept you, and the townsfolk would never accept him."

"But our differences shouldn't matter! They can make us better people. We can learn from each other."

"Yes, that's true. I wish we could live that way. But I feel the days of the free Indian are almost over. Understand this: the Indian lives with nature, and he sees no need to schedule his life and doesn't believe that what a man does in so many hours in the day is the real measure of his worth. He does what he does, and it takes as long as it takes. No one here can teach the Indian anything that would be important to him.

"The government is going to settle all the land. The attitude of white supremacy justified colonization in the first place. The Indians will have to conform and will be forced onto reservations. If they fight, they will die."

"But that's so wrong!" Rebecca ran into her room, sobbing.

"What's the matter, dear?" Ruth asked her husband, coming outside.

"It seems our daughter cares for two men from completely different backgrounds."

"Oh my," Ruth said with a moan.

# *Chapter 18*

## TIMBERLINE

WHILE the ranch hands were away getting new stock, Falling Rock came and spoke with Joel and Frederick. He asked if Rebecca could go riding with him. "Only if Frederick goes too," Joel insisted.

Rebecca saddled Butterfly and a horse for Frederick; he wasn't particular about which one he rode. The three headed up the mountain on the south side of town, along the creek Frederick had first discovered. The trek was rocky and arduous, following the animal path the Indians used. Butterfly was sure-footed and handled the terrain skillfully.

The space opened up on an expanse of marshes and lakes. Rebecca watched moose feeding in the deep water and elk along the bank. Smaller animals scurried by the trail. Flowers were everywhere, and birds filled the sky.

"Is this where you two first met?" Rebecca asked.

"Yes," Falling Rock answered. "Hunt here. No live here. This our land."

Rebecca thought about his words as they rode and remembered

what her father had said concerning the relocation of the Indians. She wondered how that would affect the Arapaho hunting grounds.

They came to a great waterfall gushing directly out of a solid rock face; the sound was nearly deafening. *How beautiful!*

As they continued to ride, the terrain grew steeper, winding between great snow-covered mountain tops. She gently urged Butterfly, who easily kept up with the other horses.

At last, they came to the top of the pass, where breathtaking images enveloped her, along with a chilly wind. Surrounding them were the tops of the snowy peaks they had seen from below. There were wetlands, small ponds formed by melting snow, and stunted trees, bare on one side and twisted by the wind. *We must be at timberline.* They stopped there to eat.

"My goodness," Rebecca said. "This is so amazing. No wonder you're trying to keep it a secret."

Falling Rock nodded without speaking.

She observed small, curious rodents and tossed them bits of bread. They took it and scurried away.

The trio continued on, going mostly downhill now, until they came to a great open meadow filled with columbines. *So this is where they grow.* She saw a herd of horses along one mountainside and a small herd of buffalo along another.

"Our people bring buffalo here many moons ago," Falling Rock said.

Then Rebecca became aware of the teepees, about a dozen of them, and the people.

# Chapter 19

## THE VISIT

TWO days later, Frederick and Rebecca came home. "Were you worried?" she asked her parents.

"A little concerned," Joel answered. "But we trust Falling Rock and knew you were safe."

"Papa," Rebecca said, sitting in the rocker next to him on the porch, "Falling Rock showed me all the land up in the mountains where his people live. He truly believes the land belongs to the Arapaho, and I think he intends to keep white people out of there. He's ever so stubborn about it."

"I see." Joel nodded as he rocked. "Eventually, that region will open to mining claims and settlers. But in the meantime, I think we can slow that process down. As mayor, I can steer the people away from that canyon by the way we design the streets. And technically, the entrance to that area is part of the claim that belongs to your brothers. We can stake off that area and mark it clearly. Hopefully that will keep trespassers out, at least for now."

"Thank you." They stood up and hugged.

The next day, Frederick and Rebecca, the whole family, including the three ranch hands, came to the big house to hear of the adventure with Falling Rock. Jonathan had just returned with the stock, and he sat in a corner, nearly out of sight.

Rebecca described the daylong journey to the Indian village, emphasizing the sights, sounds, and animals. "It's so beautiful up there and secluded. We followed the stream that feeds into Clear Creek and crossed the Continental Divide. Falling Rock's camp lies in a huge meadow surrounded by snowy peaks. He's got plenty of good water and game. Then he showed me his secret place.

"We walked a short distance through some pine trees, and running along the base of the hillside was another creek, which had carved out caves underneath the rock face. The mountain above was covered with moss, fern, small bushes, and trees. There was an animal den about halfway up the slope. The sound of water roared through the area as it plunged heedlessly downhill to the south. Falling Rock called that creek Tumbling Waters. Columbines, roses, and strawberries grew in abundance. It was heavenly." Her voice trailed off as her eyes looked up toward the ceiling. "He introduced us to his people and showed how the women worked, the men made tools, and the children played. Everyone was quite happy. I was surprised, though"—she took a breath—"that he had no wife."

Jonathan stirred, shifting his chair. Rebecca didn't notice. His face turned crimson, and he was glad to be sitting in the shadows. He had hoped Rebecca liked him, but now he wasn't sure. A fierce jealousy overwhelmed him. Would he have to fight for her?

"As we passed by the waterfall on the way back, Falling Rock said no one else was allowed on his land."

"At the town meeting," Joel said, "we agreed to mark off the entrance to that area since it is on our land. Matthew built a makeshift fence and posted signs. That's the best we can do."

"Most of the people were friendly," Frederick commented, "but I did notice a few of the braves looking at me rather suspiciously. I don't think they want war but just to be left alone. They have a good way of life; I hope they can keep it."

Rebecca remembered what her father had told her about the whites acquiring all the land.

"Well, I, for one"—Ruth stood up and hugged Rebecca tightly—"am very glad you are home!"

Matthew spoke up. "Yeah, we were just about to send out a search party for you. But Father said you would be safe, as he had talked everything over with Falling Rock before you left. And you're so independent anyway that no one could've stopped you from going."

"Yes, I'm glad we did go. It really helped me to better understand Falling Rock and his people."

Jonathan suddenly stood up and walked closer to the family. "So then, do you have feelings for him?"

"Of course I do. But I don't want to live like an Indian. I love my family and the horse ranch and this area. I want to stay here."

The group broke up. Some went outside, while Ruth and May began the task of fixing a meal.

"I've got to get back to the store." Joseph kissed May before leaving.

"I need to go visit an injured miner," Daniel said, picking up his medical bag, he rode off on his horse.

Jonathan stood close to Rebecca near the corral fence. "I'm glad you're back," he said softly. She looked up at him and smiled. He put his arms around her and kissed her.

# Chapter 20

## CHANGES

*A*S the Civil War continued in the east, things were peaceful and growing in the west. Men arrived wearing ragged uniforms. Joel thought they might have been deserters. Buildings were going up all over town: a saloon, a restaurant and hotel, a church, and a school. A stagecoach full of single ladies came to stay, and they asked the mayor, Joel, and the town council to build them a boardinghouse. Although Joel was against it, the voters approved it.

Among the single ladies was the new schoolteacher, Martha Kauffman. Matthew took an immediate liking to her, and they began courting.

Winter was mild, so construction continued as the forest kept receding. Trees were not only taken off the edges, but the larger ones were also removed. Men scouted farther up the mountain but ran into the MacKenzies' fence and turned back.

A huge deposit of silver was discovered in the range on the western side of the valley, and profiteers quickly took advantage of the find. Miners were hired to start tunnels at various sites, only to meet somewhere inside the mountain. That caused encroachment issues, forcing the smaller tunnels to be closed and the larger ones, with richer investors, to take them over. Matthew and Frederick were enraged by those actions but couldn't do anything about it. They kept their own mine, on the eastern side, to themselves.

Falling Rock visited occasionally, appalled at the development of the town. He was distressed by the decimation of the forest, the thunder of blasting, and the smoke from the smelter. Clear Creek was no longer clear. *As long as they stay away from us.*

In spring, Falling Rock brought Rebecca a basket of seeds and sprouts. "You call flowers. Plant here. Grow everywhere."

She accepted the basket and thanked him. Their eyes met, and her heart fluttered.

"Life good?" he asked.

"Yes." Tears filled her eyes. "Papa wants me to marry my foreman, Jonathan."

He studied her face and lowered his head. Without a word, he got on his horse and rode away.

She watched him disappear and then ran into her bedroom and cried.

That evening, Andrew burst into the big house, where the family gathered. "Hey, everybody, you need to come outside—now!"

May looked up from rocking Sarah. "Andrew! You don't enter a room that way!"

"But you've gotta come outside!"

Grandpa Joel stood up. "What is it?"

"C'mon." He grabbed his hand, pulling him toward the door.

May laid down a sleeping Sarah to go outside with Ruth and Rebecca.

"Look!" Andrew shouted, pointing upward. "Falling stars! Lots of 'em!"

As they stared heavenward, Joel said, "It's the Perseid meteor shower. It comes every year about this time."

"Oh, it's beautiful!" May exclaimed.

"We couldn't see it as clearly in Kentucky," Rebecca remarked. "It was never this brilliant."

"It's this massive open sky we have here," Ruth explained.

"Wow! Oh wow, there's another one!" Andrew was jumping up and down.

"It's mighty exciting," Joel said. "Quite remarkable."

Falling Rock sat cross-legged in prayer, asking for a sign of what to do about the white men moving in down the mountain. As the meteor shower began, he knew the Great Spirit was giving him that sign. Good or bad, he couldn't discern. Something was going to happen. Something was coming—and soon. He lit a small pile of brush, leaves, and herbs. Raising his arms to the sky, he swirled the smoke as an offering to the Great Spirit.

# Chapter 21

## THE ATTACK

ALLING Rock took some boys to his secret spot to teach them about the woods and animals. While there, he heard strange voices. Peering through the thick stand of pine trees, he saw six men and the glint of rifles and guns. He motioned for the children to stay quiet.

"Boy, that was a tough climb," someone said. "Do you really think we'll find any gold up here?"

"Maybe some Indians," said another.

"Well, whatever it is, we'll be ready for them." He shook his rifle in the air.

Falling Rock heard a commotion. A woman screamed, gunshots sounded, and people ran through the village, yelling. More blasts and more screaming followed, and then there was silence.

"Dobbs, let's get out of here!" someone shouted, and the six men ran past Falling Rock's hidden group, back down the path of Tumbling Waters.

Falling Rock led the frightened children to the camp, where he saw many of his people on the ground, dead and wounded. Women began to wail the death song. Blood was everywhere and on everyone. Children were crying. Burning Bear, the oldest, told the other boys, "No brave cry. We must work."

The boys helped tie up injuries, but Falling Rock didn't know how to care for gunshot wounds. Children tried to locate their families. "I'll get help," he told Burning Bear, and he mounted his horse and raced for Maysville.

Rebecca was helping Daniel arrange stock in his medical office, when Falling Rock rode up and jumped off his horse.

Rebecca gasped. "What's wrong?"

"Men come. Many guns. My people hurt bad."

Daniel and Rebecca loaded medical supplies onto their horses and hurried to the Arapaho camp with Falling Rock. They were able to get there just before evening.

"Oh my," Rebecca moaned.

"I'll need lots of hot water," Daniel ordered, and he began unloading his horse. Burning Bear and the other older boys had moved some of the injured into their teepees. Daniel went through the camp, covering bodies and assessing wounds. There were many dead men and women and even some animals.

Falling Rock and Rebecca made fires and used stone pots to heat the water. "If only you had some iron pots," she remarked, and then she heard a soft whimper and stood up.

Following the sound, she entered a teepee, where a man and woman lay dead. She waited for a moment and heard the cry again. Lifting a buffalo robe, she found a small girl. Rebecca picked her up, and the child sobbed against her breast. Rebecca took her back to the fire.

"That Rising Moon," Falling Rock said. "Here three seasons."

The little one clung to Rebecca's skirt while they worked through the night, cleaning wounds and washing equipment. Daniel operated, removing lead balls and bullets.

Falling Rock suddenly asked, "You marry Jonathan?"

Rebecca put her hands on the ground to keep from falling and stammered, "Well, no. Not yet."

"You will do?"

"I don't know now. Why?"

"Love another?" he asked.

Rebecca looked into his eyes, and the old feelings came back once again. "I don't know. Falling Rock, I really like you." She paused. "But I could never live like this. Besides, I have the horse ranch and the land to care for, and my parents need me."

"I live like you?"

She exhaled and shook her head without answering the question.

By morning, they were exhausted. Burning Bear and the other children were asleep. Rebecca laid Rising Moon on a nearby blanket and felt a stab of pain in her heart.

"It would be nice if I could get some of these people down to my office," Daniel said. "I could take better care of them there."

"Use litters for wounded," Falling Rock offered.

"I'm afraid that rocky trail is too steep for that. It would make their trauma worse. Is the way down Tumbling Waters like that also?"

Falling Rock nodded. "Many more waterfalls."

Rebecca had made some coffee for them and handed them each a cup. "Maybe I should take the children down," she said, "and send up my brothers with more supplies."

"That would be helpful," Daniel said. "I've just about run out of what we brought."

"I go?" Falling Rock asked.

"No," Daniel said, "I'll need you here since I don't know the language and to help me move the men. Burning Bear and the older boys should stay too." He looked at Rebecca and smiled with tired eyes. "She'll be safe."

"Yes, I'll be fine." She held up her gun. She then gathered up some food while the children found horses to ride. Many of them were able to ride double. Rebecca held Rising Moon next to her in the blanket, riding on Butterfly.

The MacKenzie property ran along the base of the easternmost mountains, and the busy townspeople hardly noticed them coming and going. Rebecca took the children to the big house, where Ruth and May cared for them.

After stocking their horses with food and supplies, the three brothers rode out that afternoon. Rebecca wanted to go, but Rising Moon seized her dress and began to weep. Lifting her up, she settled into the rocking chair, singing softly to her.

Daniel couldn't remember when he'd worked so hard. He exerted unfailing effort in helping Falling Rock's tribe, yet many of them died. Restless dreams brought back the terror of the people, moans of pain, screaming, and gunfire. He bolted upright from sleep, sweat pouring from his body. With his elbows on his knees, he lowered his head into his hands and wept.

Falling Rock came into the tent with some coffee Rebecca had left behind. "You work hard."

"I feel helpless. I can't make things better."

"Things are better," Falling Rock reassured him. "You save many lives."

"It's the ones I couldn't save." Daniel sighed and hung his head.

Falling Rock sat beside him and put a hand on his shoulder. "Only Great Spirit give and take. We have good life. But we not in control."

Excitement in the camp announced the three MacKenzie brothers. Frederick was furious at what he saw: the destroyed land, the carnage, and the sadness. "I'd like to hunt those people down and string them up!"

"No," Falling Rock said. "Cause more trouble. Bring more white men. We move higher."

"That will only delay another incident," Matthew said. "They'll find you again. They obsess with things they don't have, like your land."

"Yes," Joseph added, "we must make a different plan. Soldiers will come to drive you away."

"What are soldiers?" Falling Rock asked.

"Men more than the rocks on the mountain, with bigger guns than what you saw. They have authority and power to enforce their will."

Falling Rock didn't understand. He dropped to his knees and collapsed. In a dream, he saw Rebecca.

# Chapter 22

## MILITIA

*A*BE, one of the MacKenzie ranch hands, who frequently visited a lady in the boardinghouse, told her what had happened. The news spread like wildfire. Soon a mob of angry people were standing in Joel's yard. They wanted to know about the Indians and if the townspeople were in danger.

"I assure you there is no threat from them," Joel said.

"But they were attacked!" someone shouted. "They may retaliate!"

"They don't have the means to do so. They don't have guns, and many of the braves were killed."

"That could make them angry and want revenge!" someone else yelled. "They could come here and attack us." The crowd murmured in agreement.

Joel took a deep breath. "Even if they do come here, they won't bother us. We have settled this land without violence. All they want is to be left alone and live in peace."

"And remember," a woman spoke up, "they even helped us get food one winter."

"The army should come drive them away so *we* can be left alone to live in peace."

Voices became louder, with shaking fists thrust into the air.

A man rode up on his horse. "My wife is sick. Where's the doctor?"

"Up helping the Indians," someone answered.

"He should be here helping us!" He spurred his horse and rode off.

"I think we should form our own militia to protect ourselves now!"

"Folks, that won't be necessary," Joel pleaded, but he wasn't heard. The people dispersed, discussing a plan of action. Ruth came out onto the porch and hugged him. He smoothed the worry lines from her face. "This has gotten out of hand," he whispered, and he led her into the house.

In the barn, Jonathan held his own meeting. Abe, Stan, and a newer hand, Rick Madison, were there.

"We've got to form a militia—now," he said.

"I noticed several men outside who seemed interested in doing just that," Abe said.

"Couldn't that jeopardize our jobs with Mr. MacKenzie?" Rick asked.

"Not if he doesn't know who's in charge. I'm going to town for supplies, and I'll search for those men. We need to move on this quickly."

The MacKenzie ranch hands agreed and then went back to work.

Jonathan was able to locate five men to join his militia. One of the men offered his house to hold meetings. They developed a relay system to notify one another and would be prepared with loaded guns at all times in case of a surprise attack.

These actions continued to feed Jonathan's hatred.

# *Chapter 23*

## LOVE

RUTH, May, and Rebecca cared for the sixteen surviving Indian children who had come to stay with them. Rising Moon, the youngest, dominated Rebecca's affection.

Joseph came into the house with Falling Rock. "The other four boys are going to stay in camp until we can arrange for all of the people to come to the ranch," he told the women. "We can set up tents behind the house. Daniel said moving them to a new site now would be too traumatic."

Falling Rock looked around at the children and then caught Rebecca's eye. "Children good?"

"Yes," she said, "but this little one won't let me go." Rising Moon stood still on a chair while Rebecca brushed her hair.

Falling Rock said something to her in his native tongue. Rising Moon turned, grabbed Rebecca around her waist, and began to cry.

"You be mother now," he told her.

"I'm not capable of being a mother."

"She afraid of losing you."

Rebecca carried her to the rocking chair. She dried Rising Moon's face and held her tightly, speaking soft, gentle words. Soon the child was asleep.

---

Joel and Falling Rock talked well into the night about what the Indians should do. Joel explained how the army would come and put them on reservations.

"But this our land," Falling Rock protested. "We here first!"

"Yes, I know that. And I respect that. You have been very generous to us. But the government and the president, the Great White Father in Washington, want all the land to be settled. They want to collect taxes and have voters." Joel tried to explain, but Falling Rock didn't understand. He knew only that the Great Spirit had given him that land to care for.

"What is love?" Falling Rock asked.

Joel, caught off guard by the sudden change of subject, choked on his pipe smoke and looked intently at Falling Rock's earnest expression. "Love is when two people have great feelings for each other and want to spend their lives together, taking care of each other."

"Rebecca love me?"

"Well, I don't know for sure," he stated said carefully. "She certainly does have feelings for you. But she was going to marry Jonathan, our foreman."

"She say not love him."

"I see." Joel puffed on his pipe and offered it to Falling Rock. They sat in silence for a while, sharing the pipe and refilling it.

"Perhaps," Joel began as Falling Rock looked at him hopefully, "we could give you work to do. Everyone in the family has several acres. We've proven up on the land, so it is ours. Each of us could donate some adjacent land for you and your people. You could help us build houses for them and take care of our horses. You would be safe here from the soldiers and the other settlers."

"Be close to Rebecca?"

"Yes, and be close to Rebecca."

# Chapter 24

## GRACE

*A*N epic decision occurred when the MacKenzie households decided to protect the Indians. Each homestead would contribute ten acres of their land. That amounted to thirty acres for the surviving forty Indians to live on: twenty children, fifteen women, and five men, including Falling Rock.

> It is hereby decreed that the Arapaho Indian tribe, under the leadership of Falling Rock, occupy thirty acres of the MacKenzie property bordering the eastern side of the town of Maysville, Colorado Territory, under grace, including the mineral hot springs and all other resources. The land will remain the property of the MacKenzies, who will be responsible for all improvements, taxes, etc., and intended for the sole use of the Indian people. This charter is hereby executed on August 23, 1867.

The territorial governor, Alexander Hunt, signed the charter, along with Joel, Joseph, Daniel, Matthew, Frederick, and Rebecca MacKenzie. Falling Rock made an *X*.

Rebecca fashioned a sling to carry Rising Moon next to her heart.

She and Falling Rock drove a herd of horses up to the Indian camp to bring survivors to the MacKenzie property; Andrew pulled a cart behind his horse, Prince, and Mutt followed along.

The adults helped the wounded onto horses and loaded their possessions into the cart for their relocation into town. Bodies were covered and tied to horses—their sacred burial would have to wait. Most of the horses and buffalo had scattered or been killed during the attack, so there was no extra stock to move.

Andrew, now ten, stayed behind with Burning Bear, also ten, and three other boys to clean up the camp. Using shovels and brooms, the children made sure there was nothing left to tell of their existence. They covered and smoothed bloody soil, searching for artifacts and footprints. On the way down the Clear Creek side of the mountain, they covered their tracks using leafy branches.

Andrew liked moving day. He was excited to have other boys to play with and to learn their customs and teach them his.

Led by Dobbs, one of the assailants, a troop of soldiers climbed the difficult Tumbling Waters trail. When they reached the open meadow at the top, there was no sign of Indians. Scouts could find no tracks but said the soil looked disturbed. A few stray buffalo meandered around.

"You said there was a whole village here!" the captain screamed at Dobbs.

"There was! There were nearly a hunnurd when we got up here!"

"And how many did you kill?"

"Well, don't 'xactly know." Dobbs watched his foot kicking the ground. "But there were a right many braves with weapons."

Captain Anderson sighed. "Did they have guns?"

"No, sir."

"And tell me again—why were you here?"

"We was lookin' for gold, sir."

"Did they attack first?"

"Well …" He stalled. "It looked like they might. We hadda defend ourselves."

Captain Anderson glared at Dobbs. He wanted to strike him but refrained. "Troops, we will camp here for the night and go back down in the morning. If there were Indians here"—he stood in front of Dobbs with his fists on his hips—"they surely are gone now."

# Chapter 25

## SHELTER

"THIS is ridiculous," Abe complained, "having to put up tents for these heathens. Next, they'll be having us build cabins."

"What can we do about it?" Rick offered. "We are working for the MacKenzies. Does it matter what we do?"

"Of course it matters!" Jonathan fumed. "This Indian thing is becoming a habit. The MacKenzies are out of line in having us build shelters for those savages, taking care of them instead of the people in town."

"It's becoming an even bigger problem," Stan said. "They should be put on reservations now, not live here in the midst of us."

"It's frustrating," Abe said. "Who knows what they'll ask next?"

"The MacKenzies are good employers. We're making good wages," Rick said. "I've been looking for work across this country since the war ended. I don't mind helping the Indians."

"*You* don't mind!" Jonathan raged. "You're new here, so you don't know what's been going on. Do you really want those idolaters living among us?"

"I heard they believe in one Great Spirit."

"But they pray to rocks and trees and even take animal names!"

"Maybe the army will come to take them away," Stan suggested.

"That takes too long. We need to do something now!"

"I don't think Mr. MacKenzie would like that idea." Abe spoke the words carefully. He helped Rick stretch out the canvas for a tent.

"I don't really care what he likes!"

"But I thought you wanted to marry Rebecca," Stan reminded him.

"She's fallen for that pagan." Jonathan was livid. "She's pretended to show interest in me, but I think it's all a facade."

Abe picked up his hammer. "Let's just get the work done and worry about the Indians later." He drove the stake Stan was holding into the ground.

"Maybe they won't cause any trouble," Stan said.

If Jonathan's eyes had been flames of fire, he would have burned Stan to a crisp.

# Chapter 26

## LAMENT

FALLING Rock lamented the changes made to the sacred valley the MacKenzies had discovered. He thought back to the days when he last had fished there more than five seasons ago, when Clear Creek truly had been clear and cold. Now it was brown and gray, muddied up by the miners, not fit to drink. Folks were getting sick, and Daniel encouraged everyone to boil the water.

The trees were gone. Every mountainside in all four directions was laid bare to the elements; the wood was used to shore up mines and construct buildings. The air was foul with smoke. The blasting noises and the shaking ground were disturbing. He knew that now he and his people were safe from harm, yet he felt like a captive in a place where he wasn't wanted.

Falling Rock heard someone approaching and stood up.

"May I come in?" Rebecca said.

"Yes." He pulled back the tent flap.

They sat down, and she studied his face, which looked worn down with worry. He was not the handsome brave she'd met so long ago. "Are you okay? What's wrong?"

"Much wrong. Valley gone. Many people gone. Even mountain gone."

"You can still go up the mountain and hunt."

He shook his head. "You say this life better—be free. But not free in spirit."

She took his hands. "Falling Rock, I love you. I can't bear to see you hurting like this."

His face softened, and he looked into her eyes. "You love me?"

She nodded.

"You say you can't live like Indian. Now I live like white man."

"I'm sorry." Tears spilled from her eyes. "The Indian way is gone. All over the country, other tribes like yours are being rounded up and forced onto reservations to live the way the white man tells them to. But here, you are free—free to live, to hunt, to work. Your people will not be subject to the state.

"Yes, some ways have changed, but other circumstances are better. Your children will go to school. They will not be forced to stop speaking your language or practicing your customs. They will become legal American citizens, and you will work here for your support."

Rebecca's words were lost on Falling Rock. He asked, "Free to love?"

"Yes." She embraced him. "And free to love."

# Chapter 27

## TROUBLE

REBECCA brought Butterfly back to the stall after the move. Jonathan caught her by the arm. "Everything okay?" he asked. "Yes, the move was successful, and I don't think we left any telltale signs behind."

"So the Indians are going to live on your land?"

"Yes." She noticed Jonathan's look of dismay. "Anything wrong with that?"

"Plenty." He stomped off without saying goodbye.

Suddenly, Rebecca was afraid of him and what he might do to the Indians and to her.

Joel expected trouble at the next town meeting, and he got it. Most of the citizens of Maysville were outraged that Indians lived among them, even though they were on the far side of MacKenzie property.

"We've formed a militia to protect ourselves from them," someone said.

"I'm sure that won't be necessary," Joel reasoned. "Only the children will come to town, for school."

A woman screamed, "No! We can't have those savages mingling with our children!"

"I assure you they are not savage."

The crowd grew louder with complaints and accusations.

"People, this meeting is getting out of hand."

"You are the one out of hand, bringing Indians here!" someone shouted.

"Actually, they were here before we were. We just didn't see them at first."

"We need the army here to take them to a reservation!" a woman cried out.

Many agreed. "Yes!"

"We have a legal charter," Joel tried to continue. "They can stay here and work on our ranch."

Jonathan spoke up. "You care more about the Indians than your own town or us! Maybe you shouldn't be the mayor anymore!"

A meeting of the Maysville militia was held. Jonathan Adams became the newly elected leader. He raged at his volunteers. "How dare the MacKenzies give land to the Indians that rightfully belongs to white settlers?" The crowd rose in an uproar. "And, men," he goaded them on, "we must take action in an orderly fashion, not as a riotous mob. So if any Indians leave their land, they must be shot on sight as trespassers. Besides, there has got to be another way up the mountain than the one the MacKenzies have fenced off. I'll take two men with me to go find another trail."

Abe and Stan agreed to go. After more discussion and planning, the men began to dissipate.

In his heart, Jonathan dismissed his intention of marrying Rebecca and inheriting her homestead.

"It's crucial we get those Indians out of here," Jonathan said as the three ranch hands returned from their search. "We'll have to trap them somehow to get them to fight, and then we can force the army to come take them away."

"Well, we couldn't find their camp in the mountains," Abe said.

"There was no trace of them," Stan continued. "All we did find was plenty of places to try to mine, hunt, and live."

"There's no evidence because the Indians are here!" Jonathan screeched. "They are bound to cause trouble sooner or later."

"Not with the MacKenzies protecting them."

"What—are you on their side now?" Jonathan grabbed Stan.

"No, they just don't seem like the type to cause trouble."

"They've just been brutally attacked," Abe added, "and there's hardly any of them left."

"Then I guess we'll just have to create some trouble for them," Jonathan said.

"Won't that make us look bad?" Stan asked.

"Not if we handle it right," Jonathan explained. "It has to look like they start the trouble. We have a new law that says any Indian who steps off MacKenzie property can be shot on sight. We just need to find a way to make that happen."

"What excuse can we use to have one of them come to town?" Abe asked.

"Maybe"—Jonathan paced with his hand on his chin—"somebody will need a doctor."

# Chapter 28

## JEALOUSY

REBECCA went to Falling Rock's tent to warn him of the possible danger from Jonathan.

"Rebecca!"

"It's Jonathan," she told Falling Rock. She dropped her embrace just as Jonathan barged into the tent.

"What are you doing here?" He glared at her.

"Just visiting," she replied casually.

"Looks like more than that to me!" Jonathan gripped Falling Rock's shirt with his left hand, making a fist with his right. "We are to be married; you leave her alone!"

"She no love you." Falling Rock stayed calm.

"What? Did she tell you that?"

"Jonathan." Rebecca tried to break his grip. "Stop this now!"

"Oh, yes, ma'am." He dropped his hold but kept both arms raised close to his chest with fists clenched, ready to fight. "Since you're the boss and all."

"My father's the boss. Besides, I heard you started a militia organization in opposition to his will."

"I'm protecting the town against these savages." He scowled. "They're causing trouble all over the country. They need to be put on a reservation."

"No, they don't!" Rebecca stamped her foot. "They will live here and work for our family."

"And what about us?" Jonathan asked Rebecca while still fixing an angry stare on Falling Rock.

"We should talk about this outside."

"No! I want the truth right here right now! What did he mean when he said you don't love me?"

"I may not ..." She hesitated and looked at Falling Rock. "Love you anymore."

Jonathan seized Falling Rock by the shoulders. "Do you think she could love you, an uncultured heathen?"

Falling Rock was dismayed. There were still many English words he didn't understand, but recognizing rage and jealousy, he kept quiet.

Jonathan shook Falling Rock vigorously. "Well? Speak up! I heard you've been learning English!"

"Jonathan, stop it!" Rebecca shouted. "Let him go."

He released Falling Rock and turned his attack toward her. "And what about you? You would marry this uncivilized barbarian and raise half-breed children?"

Her face flushed.

"I've never seen someone so shameless!" Jonathan struck her with a right backhand, knocking her down. His ring scraped her face.

Falling Rock grabbed him, picked him up, and threw him out of the tent. "You leave here. My place. My woman."

The right side of Rebecca's face showed swelling and bleeding where the ring had cut her skin. "I'm so glad you didn't hit him." She tried to smile as Falling Rock lifted her from the ground and carried her to her parents' home.

# Chapter 29

## INJURY

"OH my." Ruth gasped when she opened the door to Falling Rock carrying Rebecca. "Come in, and follow me. Lay her on the bed." Ruth wrapped Rebecca up in her childhood quilt. "Go get Daniel," she ordered.

Without hesitation, Falling Rock left the MacKenzie property and ran through town to Daniel's office.

"Rebecca hurt bad," he explained.

"How?"

"Jonathan."

Daniel grabbed his medical bag and jumped onto his horse.

As Falling Rock watched him ride away, he heard footsteps.

"Well, lookee what we got here."

Falling Rock turned to face Jonathan.

"Fellas, looks like we've got ourselves an Indian trespassing in our town." Jonathan raised his gun and aimed at Falling Rock. "Just what is the new law?"

"Shoot him on sight!" the militiamen shouted as they drew their weapons.

"Stop this immediately!" Joel MacKenzie shouted, riding up to the group. "What's going on here?"

"We caught this Injun trespassin' off your land," Abe pointed out.

"Rebecca hurt bad," Falling Rock told Joel.

"Get on!" Joel grabbed Falling Rock's arm, pulling him onto his horse. "You men put those guns away and disperse right now!" Joel turned his back on the crowd as they galloped away.

"Just who are we going to listen to?" Jonathan asked. He aimed his gun and fired but threw it onto the ground when he thought they'd ridden out of range.

Joel found Frederick and asked him to go to Golden to telegraph for a marshal as he and Falling Rock rushed home.

Joel burst into the house. "How is she?"

"Shh!" Ruth scolded him. "Daniel's in with her now."

Falling Rock came in silently. Joel turned to him and asked, "What happened?"

As Falling Rock shared the details of Jonathan's attack, Ruth said, "You're bleeding!"

"It appears," Joel stated, "that Jonathan's vile intentions were aimed at you too." He examined Falling Rock's arm. "The bullet just grazed you. Get something to wrap this up."

Ruth got a basin of water to clean the wound and wrapped it with a cloth. She sat with the men to await Daniel's report.

"This will not go unpunished!" Joel murmured, gritting his teeth. "And Jonathan was such a good worker too. I even thought he and Rebecca ..." He stopped short, looking at Falling Rock. "I've sent Frederick to Golden for the marshal. We've got to get some law and order up here. This militia thing is out of control."

Daniel came out of Rebecca's bedroom, quietly closing the door behind him. "I gave her some laudanum so she could get some sleep."

Joel was on his feet. "What about her injuries?"

"The swelling could use some ice, if we had any. We probably need to build an icehouse and cut blocks from the creek this winter. Her face is going to bruise badly. Mother, could you put a cold compress on her?"

"Yes, but—" Joel was impatient. He noticed blood on the front of Falling Rock's shirt. "Where did that blood come from?"

"She has a very bad cut on her right cheek. It required a couple of stitches," Daniel said. In the background, Ruth caught her breath as she took a bowl of water into Rebecca's room. "And one of her teeth was nearly knocked out."

"I'll knock *his* teeth out." Joel made a fist and headed for the door.

"No," Daniel insisted. "We must wait for the marshal. I'll make a full report."

Joel sat down again while Daniel unwrapped Falling Rock's arm.

"My fault," Falling Rock moaned.

"How is it your fault?" Joel exclaimed.

"I say she not love him."

"That was pretty obvious without your having to say it," Joel stated. "As for him forming a militia, that was totally uncalled for. He's way out of line here. Hopefully the marshal will see it that way too."

Daniel finished dressing Falling Rock's wound. "It may hurt for a while."

"No more hurt than my heart."

Rebecca awoke while the marshal talked with Joel and Daniel. Rising Moon was allowed in, and she lay on the bed next to Rebecca. Falling Rock stood in the doorway.

"Come in," Rebecca invited. "Sit down." He took the chair by her writing desk.

They sat for a while without speaking. Overcome with regret, she confessed to him. "Oh, Falling Rock, I'm so sorry for what we have done to your land."

"Not you. Others."

"But if we hadn't come here and found everything so beautiful and luxuriant."

"What mean *lux*—"

"Abundant vegetation. Thick with pine trees. Plenty of game. Now look at it: the trees are gone, and the water is polluted, and me-" She gingerly touched her cheek. "And I'm not beautiful anymore either." She let tears slide down her damaged face.

Falling Rock went over to her and lifted her chin. "You beautiful here." He touched her heart. "I glad you come."

"But your land."

"Others do it, not you."

"Oh, Falling Rock." She began to sob.

He pulled her close and kissed her forehead. Rising Moon snuggled nearby.

They heard a knock on the door, and Falling Rock stepped back.

"I brought you this to make you feel better," Ruth said, blushing, "but I see you're already feeling better." She placed a tray with tea and toast on the desk and left.

# Chapter 30

## REVENGE

BACK on MacKenzie land, the four ranch hands discussed the situation.

"You'd better skedaddle," Abe suggested to Jonathan. "Mr. MacKenzie isn't going to let this go, and I've heard he's ordered a U.S. marshal to come up here."

"Let him come," Jonathan was cocky. "I'll tell them how much trouble the Indians have made."

"But they haven't made any trouble," Stan reminded him.

"Just whose side are you on?"

"I'm only saying they sustained a violent attack without fighting back, then quietly moved to the ranch. They're not even in town."

Jonathan punched Stan hard, knocking the wind out of him, causing him to collapse. "Then maybe you should go with them!"

"Jonathan, you're being unreasonable," Rick said.

"What's going on here?" Jonathan shouted. "I'm in charge of this militia!"

"I'm not so sure we need one," Abe said helping Stan up off the ground. "Maybe the one we need protection from is *you!*"

Red-faced with rage, Jonathan grabbed the nearest animal and jumped on. He rode off with Rebecca's horse, Butterfly.

# Chapter 31

## LONELINESS

REBECCA was outside with Falling Rock when Butterfly returned. The horse was limping, having thrown Jonathan into a mine-tailings pile and slipping on the loose rock. Jonathan's body was discovered the next day with a broken neck.

"Something's wrong with Butterfly," Rebecca told Falling Rock.

Cooing softly, he passed his hands gently over the horse's shoulder, moving down her leg. Butterfly began to tremble as he got nearer to the painful area. She snorted and jerked her head. Falling Rock stepped back until she was calm. Rebecca smoothed her forelock, singing quietly. Falling Rock again approached, speaking loving reassurance in his Indian tongue and touching her leg. Butterfly stood still, wincing, but let him examine it.

He had tears in his eyes when he rose and looked at Rebecca.

"What is it?" She was afraid to ask.

"Leg broken."

"No!" she screamed, clutching Butterfly's neck. Sobbing into her mane, she repeated, "No, no. Oh, my poor beautiful Butterfly."

Falling Rock gradually eased her grip. After one last look at Rebecca, Butterfly closed her eyes, as if knowing her fate.

Rebecca ran into the house, ignored her mother's inquiry, pushed Rising Moon away, closed her bedroom door, and fell down onto the bed. She cried until she was startled alert when she heard the gunshot.

She went to her desk, picked up her red velvet journal, and read the last page. It was full of hope and joy, dreams of adventure, and love for Falling Rock.

She lifted her pen, dipped it into the inkwell, and began to write of the recent events, beginning with the assault by Jonathan and the loss of Butterfly. A teardrop fell onto the page over the words *broken heart*.

Rebecca had never felt truly alone. With four older brothers, a sister-in-law, a niece and nephew, her parents, and several ranch hands, she never had known what loneliness was—until the loss of Butterfly.

Back in Kentucky, she'd been able to go out riding by herself with her beautiful palomino horse, whom she considered her best friend. She'd packed food and been gone from sunup until sundown, and her parents never had worried. Rebecca had been the first one to handle Butterfly when she was born. No one else had managed her training.

In rugged Colorado, there were no trails. She had ridden with Andrew around the ranch area and with Falling Rock, who knew the way above the valley. With everyone working so hard to prove up on the homesteads, establish the ranch, clear the land for crops, and carve out the side of a mountain, no one seemed to have time for her.

She opened the trunk her grandmother had given her and placed Butterfly's lead rope, halter, bridle, and reins inside, along with the leather-riding crop. Then she laid her journal on top and closed the lid. There were no more tears left to cry. She took a deep breath and stood up, knowing that whatever she had to do from now on, she had to do it alone.

When she came out of her room, Falling Rock was sitting at the table, talking to Ruth and Joel. The three stood up. Rebecca wanted to run into her mother's arms, as she had as a child, but she took another deep breath instead.

"Come. Walk," Falling Rock invited, holding out a hand.

After they left, Ruth told Joel, "Sometimes you just need to cry."

Falling Rock led Rebecca on an unfamiliar route. At the top, they stood close together, surveying the Clear Creek valley and all the activity. At the ranch in the east, it was quiet.

They continued over the hill, until they came to a great open meadow filled with blue and purple columbines. *So they grow here too.*

They sat under a tree for a while without speaking, and then Rebecca said, "Oh, Falling Rock, I'm so sorry for what we have done to you and your land."

"Not you. Others."

"But we found it and led them here." She began to cry.

He pulled her close, covered her mouth with a finger, and then kissed her.

To ensure their safety, Falling Rock and Rebecca drove a wagon with the native children from the ranch to the one-room school building and picked them up again.

Martha Kauffman MacKenzie taught two classes in Maysville: one for the local settlers' children from eight until noon and another for the Indian children from one to four o'clock. She was dismayed that folks insisted the classes be segregated. *Maybe in time, they will be accepted.*

Andrew elected to go to school with his best friend, Burning Bear.

He became a teacher's assistant, helping the Indian children learn English. Once they could read and write, they studied US government and what was required to become an American citizen. Later, the Indian Citizen Act of 1924 finally would recognize natives as citizens, and the Indian Reorganization Act of 1934 would give them full rights to land, housing, and economic self-sufficiency.

Andrew and Burning Bear were together all the time. They helped out on the ranch and played in the shallow pools off Clear Creek with Mutt. They knew not to go into the main current.

Andrew showed Burning Bear his colt, Prince. "You should have a colt too."

Rebecca was walking through the corral with an armful of hay, when Andrew asked, "Aunt Rebecca, is there another colt that Burning Bear could have?"

"Soon we'll have a couple more," she said, taking the hay to the barn.

"How long is *soon*?" Burning Bear asked Andrew.

"I don't know, but soon."

# Chapter 32

## THE ARMY

THE army came to Maysville and stopped at the MacKenzie ranch. Joel opened the door and stepped outside.

"Good day, Mr. MacKenzie. I'm Captain Anderson. We understand you are harboring some Indians."

"No, you are incorrect. There are some Indians living and working on my ranch. They were here on this land before we came."

"This is US government land, and I have an order here to relocate the Indians onto a reservation."

"I'm sorry." Joel stood firm. "You are incorrect again. This is my land, on a proven-up homestead. I can hire anyone I wish."

"You don't realize the danger you are in from these hostile savages."

"These people are neither hostile nor savage. They are working, earning their keep, and learning English and American law, such as the Declaration of Independence, which says that all men are created equal. I don't know where you got your information from, but everything you've told me is incorrect."

Captain Anderson blustered. His red face glowed. "Look, Mr. MacKenzie, I've already investigated the other side of the mountain, going up the Tumbling Waters trail. I know there was an Indian attack, and I know there were survivors."

"You mean, sir, that the Indians were attacked. More than half their tribe was massacred, but they didn't retaliate. They quietly, without incident, moved into Maysville, onto my property. I have a copy of the legal charter here, if you'd like to examine it." He handed him the document.

The captain glanced at it. "This means nothing!" He threw it onto the ground. "It only proves that you do indeed have forty Indians here. I've seen this document in Denver City, and that's why I'm here—to collect those Indians."

"I'm sorry, but you have no jurisdiction here. You may take it up with the federal marshal if you like, but I suggest you leave now."

Flustered and empty-handed, Captain Anderson motioned for his troop to mount their horses and prepare to depart. He glared at Joel. "This is not over yet!"

Rebecca came alongside her father. "What was that all about?"

"They are trying to remove Falling Rock and his people and take them to a reservation. But our charter is legal and binding. They can't do anything about it."

Rebecca turned and saw Falling Rock. "I make trouble for you," he said."

"No, they make trouble for themselves," Rebecca answered. "Everything is all right. This is your home. You are protected here, and no one can change that. Someday the government will grant Indians the same rights we have, but until then, we will protect you and stand up for you."

"Not my way to hide."

"You are not hiding! You are living!" Joel spoke up. "I've heard of the terrible conditions on these reservations: no food, water, decent clothes, or housing. You are much better off here. We will get this straightened out." He reached out to shake Falling Rock's hand.

"You boss." Falling Rock took his hand. "Now work." He walked off with Rebecca.

"What's happening?" Ruth asked.

"The army is trying to take Falling Rock's people. Our charter was filed with the territorial governor at the time, Alexander Hunt. The current governor, Edward McCook, signed the order Captain Anderson had. He was one of the Fighting McCooks during the Civil War and has quite a reputation. I don't know how much trouble we may get from him. We may have to go to court."

"Oh dear." Ruth sighed. "I sure hope it won't come to that."

Joel hugged his wife. "Me too."

Joel hired an attorney, who studied both documents. "The original charter is binding," he said. "Any motion in court would be thrown out."

# *Chapter 33*

## COLUMBINE

SWEAT poured from Falling Rock as he struggled with the birth of the foal. Rebecca could only see his elbows as she tried to comfort the mare and keep her still.

"It coming," he said, panting, and he turned the animal while he pulled against the strain, until two hoofs appeared in his hands. With one final heave, the baby slid out onto the hay. "Not breathing." He looked up at Rebecca.

"No!" She leaped forward and began clearing the nose and mouth. "Press on her chest." Soon the filly snorted and shook her head. Rebecca rubbed her down and eased her to the mare. "Good girl," she cooed. "You're going to be all right."

They washed their hands together in a bucket, and Falling Rock took hers in his. "You need to be all right. You need to love again."

"I couldn't. I just couldn't. No one could replace Butterfly."

They watched the foal nurse. "Much work but good horse." He looked at Rebecca. "This one you love?"

Rebecca was incredulous. "Oh, I don't know."

He touched her shoulder. "Soon pain better. I too hurt from loss."

She looked at him, and he smiled. She threw her arms around him. "Oh, Falling Rock." She sobbed in his arms.

He stroked her long hair. "It okay." He held her. There were no more words to say.

The mare and foal were on their feet by the end of the day. Falling Rock brushed the mother and spoke with a soothing voice. Andrew and Burning Bear came into the barn to see them.

"This will be yours," Andrew told his friend. "I promised Burning Bear a horse."

"Not this one. Is Rebecca's."

"Oh." Andrew kicked his foot into the dirt. "We'll have many more horses," he told Burning Bear. "Aunt Rebecca is raising them to sell."

"She doesn't mind if I get one?"

"Not at all. You are part of our family. Then we can go riding together. Come on." The boys ran off with Mutt, looking for some adventure.

Rebecca and Rising Moon came with a carrot. Rebecca told the mare, "You're beautiful, and you had a beautiful baby."

The mare shook her mane and took the carrot from the girl. Rebecca knelt down to pet the filly.

"This your horse," Falling Rock said. "I know. Great Spirit tell me."

She looked up at him. "Really?"

"Yes. You give name."

The curious animal looked into her eyes. Compassion flowed through Rebecca. "Columbine," she whispered. The filly tossed her head in response. "Yes, Columbine." Rebecca hugged her neck while Falling Rock nodded in agreement.

# EPILOGUE

ON August 1, 1879, the Territory of Colorado became the thirty-eighth state of the Union. Maysville was made the county seat of Clear Creek County.

Mining on the west side of town halted, in many cases due to cross-filing of claims and unlawful intrusion into tunnels. The MacKenzies' tunnels on the east side were not affected and produced high volumes of minerals. When the Sherman Silver Act of 1890 changed currency to the gold standard, many people lost their fortunes and left Maysville, leaving behind their beautiful Victorian mansions.

Even though the MacKenzies prospered, the town remained small. The train shipped out ores until mining played out and then brought tourists for hunting and fishing expeditions. Matthew and Frederick operated a guide and outfitting business. Stores and shops began, but most didn't last long.

Cabins that could withstand the harsh weather conditions were built on the southeastern corner of MacKenzie property to house the Indians.

Joel and Ruth began to feel their age and the cold more severely. Joel resigned as mayor, and their children cared for them as it became necessary.

Joseph and May continued to run the store, with Andrew helping occasionally, although he preferred going to school and playing with his Indian friends. Sarah liked working with her grandma in the warm kitchen of the big house, cooking and sewing. After they lost their second son, May had no more babies.

Daniel was busy running his medical office and added a wing for use as a hospital. He hired a nurse, Donna Bradley, to assist him. They shared off time together while courting.

Matthew and Martha had twin boys, Mark and Luke. Martha continued to teach school, while Matthew worked with his brother Frederick, who remained a bachelor.

Rebecca and Falling Rock married and lived in the big house so they could operate the horse ranch. They raised prize Kentucky thoroughbreds, along with their five children and Rising Moon.

Hired labor and ranch hands worked the horses and cattle, cultivated hay, and gardened. The greenhouse produced vegetables all year long.

Rick Madison stayed on at the MacKenzie ranch and eventually married Rising Moon. Burning Bear married Sarah.

All the while, the trees grew back on the mountains, and Clear Creek flowed clear once again.

Blossom Rock Quartz

Gold Ore on Blossom Rock

Bless't Pair of Quartz

Gold Ore on Ironstone Rock

Printed in the United States
by Baker & Taylor Publisher Services